GENERAL MUSTER

&

NO-TREES TOWN

D1114591

Book 1 – Tuff, Sadie & The Wild West
Book 2 – General Muster & No-Trees Town

Coming soon:

Book 3 – Grizzly Bears & Beaver Pelts
Book 4 – Macho Nacho & The Cowboy Battle
Book 5 – The Parrot Gang & Wild West Ghosts
Book 6 – The Nasty Boys & The Bobbies
Book 7 – Judge Roy Bean & Wild Thing

To Vy Nguyen,

GENERAL MUSTER & NO-TREES TOWN

Hideout Kids Book 2

by Mike Gleason

Illustrated by Victoria Taylor

FARM STREET PUBLISHING

First published 2017 by Farm Street Publishing
www.hideoutkidsbooks.com

Paperback ISBN 978-1-912207-03-9
Hardback ISBN 978-1-912207-04-6
eBook ISBN 978-1-912207-05-3

A CIP catalogue record for this book is available from
the British Library.

Design and typesetting by Head & Heart

To Michelle and Luke,
who inspired me to write these stories
of the Wild West.

TUFF

SADIE

WILD THING

CONTENTS

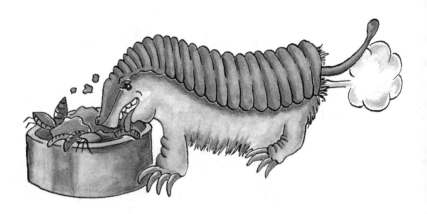

JUDGE
JUNE'S
HUT

Dear Reader,

General Muster & No-Trees Town is the second in the series of Hideout Kids books.

There was a good reason the Wild West was "wild". Many of the Americans who moved to the American Frontier didn't behave very well. Bad behavior often meant that the United States Army had to be called in to help bring order and force outlaws to obey the laws.

In this amazing story, a vicious army of outlaws surrounds Muleshoe, the home of the Hideout Kids. Because only children can find Muleshoe, Judge June sends Sheriff Tuff and Deputy Sadie to guide a United States Army General, so he can build an Army camp to help protect the town.

If you want to curl up with a good story, start curling and turn the page.

Mike Gleason

TUFF AND SADIE'S JOURNEY TO MEET GENERAL MUSTER

INDIAN TERRITORY

Sweetwater

TEXAS

Horsehead Canyon

Colorado River

GULF OF MEXICO

Rio Grande River

GENERAL MUSTER

&

NO-TREES TOWN

CHAPTER ONE

DRAW, SHERIFF

It was high noon on a boiling hot summer day in Muleshoe.

On the dusty main road, Sheriff Tuff Brunson squared his shoulders. He stood ramrod straight as he faced "Big Nose" George Parrot, the meanest outlaw in the Wild West.

Tuff stared straight into the vicious outlaw's bloodshot eyes. "I won't tolerate teenage gang members in this town," Tuff said, in a voice barely above a whisper. "Drop your water blaster and walk away. Now."

Big Nose George wiped the sweat from his brow. "Draw," he growled through his black-stained yellow teeth. "Muleshoe don't have room for the both of us."

Tuff curled his fingers around his bullwhip, hoping he would be lucky with it again this time.

"Look out, you dirty outlaw, here comes Sheriff Tuff Brunson!" he cried as he whirled the bullwhip out.

"CRACK!" He whipped Big Nose George's super soaker from its holster.

"Don't mess with the fastest whip in the West," Tuff said, hiding his relief.

Deputy Dan Pigeon pounced on Big Nose George and pulled his arms up tight behind his back.

"Put handcuffs on that ugly bandit then throw him in jail," Tuff said as he waved his bullwhip in the air. "Be careful he doesn't try anything sneaky."

"Nice one," said Tuff's deputy Sadie

Marcus, as she smiled at him from beneath her wide-brimmed hat. She watched from the veranda of the Happy Days Saloon. "He didn't even get close to his squirter. Hey, look out, Tuff."

Tuff heard the scrape of boots on dust behind him. He whirled around. Big Nose George had tried to wrestle the handcuffs away from Deputy Dan.

"CRACK!" Tuff's whip leapt out. The whip curled and snapped as it wrapped in a knot around Big Nose George and pinned his arms to his side.

"Now that rascal is roped good and tight, cuff him up," Tuff said.

Deputy Dan yanked Big Nose George's wrists together, shoved them into the handcuffs and clicked them shut.

"Look at this," laughed Deputy Dan as he took Big Nose George's water gun away. "This wasn't loaded with water. He had bubble-gum instead. Watch." Deputy Dan pulled the trigger and a big pink bubble popped out of the barrel.

"I'm not surprised," said Sadie. "The Parrots are dumb."

"You might have got me now, Sheriff Brunson, but you won't keep me long in that chicken-pen jail of yours," hollered Big Nose George. "My sister 'Tiny Nose' Peggy has got a big surprise for you. You and your snotty-nosed dep-u-ty are gonna get what you deserve."

"It's not a chicken pen, it's a parrot pen. See ya later, Big Mouth Parrot," Tuff laughed, as he rolled up his whip and hung it on his belt.

"Crime doesn't pay, does it?" said Sadie with a grin. "Poor Big Nose George. He's not as scary as he thinks. Let's go get a sarsaparilla. Judge June will be in the saloon. She might have a job for us."

As Tuff and Sadie walked toward the saloon doors, the tiny cowboy poet appeared at the end of the veranda. "Look, Tuff, there's our little singing friend," Sadie whispered. The little cowboy sat in his old rocking chair, his boots propped up on the rail, as he sang,

Big Nose George will cry
Since he's back in jail
But the Parrots know
It's not the end of the tale

An army of outlaws
Threatens Muleshoe
Unless help arrives
What will the kids do?

"Hey, cowboy –" Tuff started to say, but the tiny cowboy had disappeared.

Tuff and Sadie pushed open the batwing doors and walked into the noisy Happy Days Saloon.

The saloon was crowded with Muleshoe

children eating lunch. The air smelled of *cabrito* – barbequed goat. Judge Junia "June" Beak had one arm propped on the wooden bar as she talked with Toothless Tom, the bartender.

Tuff and Sadie weaved their way through the tables to Judge June, who raised her hand to stop them. "There's not time for a sarsaparilla," she said. "I have a job for you. Someone very important is coming to Muleshoe and I need to make sure he gets here safely. Let's go over to the hut and talk. There are way too many ears listening around here."

Tuff saw "Little Nose" George Parrot at a nearby table.

"What are you doing here, birdbrain?" Tuff said to him. "Would you like to join your big brother in the bird cage?"

Little Nose George took off his filthy black hat as he glared at Tuff. "You're no worry to The Parrot Gang," he snarled. "My brother will be out of jail before you can say 'boo'. Me and my sister Tiny Nose Peggy are about to take over this town. We've got an outlaw army."

"Oh, go jump in a lake, 'Little Brain' George," said Judge June. "C'mon kids, let's get over to the hut."

CHAPTER TWO

A JOB IN THE SAND HILLS

Tuff squinted in the hot sunshine as they walked across the dusty road and through the bright yellow door of Judge June's hut. They felt the magical air of Judge June's den as she closed the door behind them.

Tuff and Sadie looked around the room. Maps lined the walls and books were stacked in piles on the floor.

A huge black bear stood in a corner. It had scary white eyes and sharp bared teeth.

Thank goodness, he's dead and stuffed, thought Tuff. *Wait, did that bear look at me?* He shuddered.

Judge June's pet pink fairy armadillo, Wild Thing, snored in her bed but sat straight up when they sat down in the chairs around Judge June's desk. "Grr," she growled, "did you bring me any mash?"

"Sure, here you go, precious," said Sadie as she put a huge bowl of crushed locusts and maggots in front of Wild Thing. "Don't chew with your mouth open."

"OK," said Wild Thing as she let out a massive burp that filled the room with the smell of stinky cheese.

"That's disgusting," said Sadie as she pinched her nose.

"Think so?" Wild Thing said. "How about this?" She blew out a massive bomb of an armadillo toot, which stank like a barn full of 400 goats with diarrhea.

"Please, Wild Thing," Judge June said. "Sorry, kids. Wild Thing's jealous. Until you arrived she called herself the Sheriff of Muleshoe."

"Yeah," snarled Wild Thing. "Now you

two have taken over. I'm mad. Unless you feed me lots of mash. Now give me more."

"OK, darling," Sadie said. "Here's a nice bowl of mashed-up fleas, bees, mosquitoes and yellow jackets."

Sadie has a soft spot for the little critter, thought Tuff.

"CHOMP!" went Wild Thing and ignored the children.

"The job I have for you is dangerous," Judge June continued in a low voice. "A United States Army brigade led by General 'Buster' Muster is on its way to Muleshoe. I've asked him to build an army camp near The Big Spring."

Sadie asked, "Have you mapped out the General's trail? Will they come over the Sand Hills?"

"Yes. Here's the map," Judge June said as she laid it on her desk. "When they get to Horsehead Canyon, they'll enter the Sand Hills."

"There are lots of hiding places in those Sand Hills," said Tuff. "They're full of danger."

"Your job is to join their wagon train at Horsehead Canyon, then ride with them all the way into Muleshoe. General Muster's a grown-up and won't be able to find Muleshoe without your help," Judge June said. "You must move fast because Tiny Nose Peggy Parrot has gathered together a mass of outlaw gangs outside The Big Spring. You only have two days to get the General here. If you don't make it, Muleshoe might be taken over by the outlaws."

"So what Little Nose George told us was true," Tuff said.

"Yes," said Judge June. "Don't forget, the Parrots lived in Muleshoe when they were children. Now that they're teenagers, they still know how to find the town, and want the outlaw gangs to take over. With help from the US Army, we'll be able to stop them."

Tuff stared hard at the map. "It's a long way

to go in two days. I'm sure the gangs will be out to stop us."

"Don't worry," said Sadie, "with our bullwhips, we can fight off anybody."

"I know," said Tuff, "but what if that nasty Sam Bass and his gang are around? He's the leader of the outlaw gangs."

"Look," said Judge June. "Any of the gangs might try to stop you. General Muster doesn't

know the area as well as you. If you stick to the trail and don't wander off, you should be fine."

"Alright then," said Tuff. He reached down and felt the warm handle of his trusty bullwhip. "I'm ready."

"I better go with 'em," Wild Thing shouted, sensing an adventure. "They're new at this job. They need my muscles and giant brain."

"Your brain is the size of a pea but your mouth is the size of a whale. Please be quiet," Judge June said.

"Grr," growled Wild Thing as she curled up and went back to sleep. She was fierce but also very, very lazy.

"Good," said Judge June. "Now, both of you close your eyes, and don't say a word. I'll give you something to help you on the journey."

As Tuff and Sadie closed their eyes, Judge June raised her arms toward the sky and quietly chanted a spell.

"You may open your eyes now," said the magical judge, as she gazed at them with her almond-shaped blue-gray eyes. "I'm a good witch, and use my power to protect the children of Muleshoe. But to fight the outlaws we must have help from the US Army. Take the map with you. It shows all of the landmarks and towns along the way," she said. "Remember, it's easier to *stay* out of trouble than to *get* out of trouble. Be careful."

CHAPTER THREE

A STOP IN SWEETWATER TOWN

The next morning, Tuff woke to hear his favorite bird, the mockingbird, sing like a red-tailed hawk. He loved mockingbirds. They copied, or mocked, the songs of other birds.

The early morning sun shimmered off the dew on the mesquite trees as Tuff and Sadie walked into the stables and saddled up their horses.

"I hope Silver Heels and Jenny had plenty of rest," Tuff said. "This will be a long ride. Hey Sadie," he added. "What did you put in your saddlebags?"

"Some fresh white sheets," answered Sadie. "I don't like to sleep in my bedroll without a clean sheet. I borrowed them from Judge June."

Tuff wondered why. He liked to sleep in his bedroll as it was. "You didn't borrow them. I bet you took them."

"That's none of your business," Sadie said. "By the way, what will you do about that pygmy rattlesnake behind you?"

"What the –?"

He looked down at the hay-covered stable floor. To his horror, Tuff was eye to eye with a coiled western pygmy rattlesnake, the most dangerous of all of the Texas rattlers.

"RATTLE RATTLE!"

"NEIGH!" Sadie's horse Jenny exploded with noise and stomped as she stared down the snake. "Get out of here you slimy reptile," Jenny snorted.

Tuff and Sadie watched Jenny work the mean brown rattler with the long red mark down its spine into a nearby gopher hole.

"Good girl," Sadie said as she gave Jenny a pat and some sugar cubes. "Isn't it fun to protect the boys?"

"They always need to be looked after," neighed Jenny as she winked at Silver Heels.

Tuff and Sadie donned their white hats and mounted up for the long ride ahead.

"Let's make the first watering hole, over near Sweetwater Town, by sunset," Tuff said as they trotted out of Muleshoe. "There's an old cow camp there where we can bed down for the night. Tomorrow we'll get these horses on a fast gallop so we get to Horsehead Canyon by lunchtime."

"What do you know about General Muster?" Sadie said as she slipped her boots into the stirrups.

"I know he's cracked down on all the lawlessness in Texas."

"I bet he's got a lot of enemies."

"I think there's something else that gives him enemies," Tuff said. "He used to be an outlaw. The General's not afraid to protect himself."

Late in the afternoon, Tuff and Sadie reined in their steeds as they rode into Sweetwater Town. A bunch of unfriendly faces stared at them as they passed through the narrow main road.

"It could be some of the outlaw gangs stay

here while they wait to invade Muleshoe," Tuff said.

He had an uneasy feeling while they unpacked their saddlebags and made supper of venison sausages and prairie chicken eggs.

"Something doesn't feel right about this town," he said. "Let's sleep with one eye open tonight."

"I brought some dice with me," Sadie said. "Let's play a quick game of 'chuck-a-luck' so I can win all your money."

Sadie pulled out her dice and square cage and rolled three sixes.

"Hey, those are loaded dice," Tuff said with a laugh. "You're up to your tricks, Sadie."

After the dice game was over they bedded down under a blanket of stars. Tuff still had a worried feeling.

It didn't help that a pack of coyotes, the wild prairie wolves, howled nearby.

I wonder if we're being watched, he thought as he kept one eye open.

CHAPTER FOUR

MEET GENERAL "BUSTER" MUSTER

The next morning, Tuff and Sadie woke with the rising sun. "It's going to be another hot day," Tuff said. "Let's make sure the horses have plenty of water."

"I'm glad we had a quiet night," Sadie said.

"Yeah, but I'm pretty sure I saw someone circle our camp all night," Tuff said. "Let's ride out of here fast."

"Giddy-up Silver Heels. C'mon Jenny," Tuff and Sadie shouted as they spurred their horses and rode out of Sweetwater Town in a cloud of dust.

Tuff led the way as they galloped across the High Plains through the summer heat. It wasn't long before they spotted a wagon train moving toward them.

"It must be the General," said Tuff.

The wagon train rolled along the Goodnight-Loving Trail towards Horsehead Canyon. Tuff counted two wagons.

As Tuff and Sadie slowed their horses, a lone rider approached. "Where's the US Army brigade?" Tuff asked Sadie.

The rider pulled up next to them.

"You must be Tuff and Sadie. I'm the Wagon Boss," he said. "Judge June told General Muster you would meet us. We're glad you're here; come meet the General."

They followed the Wagon Boss to the

front wagon, which had a rifle-toting cowboy riding on top. The cowboy wore a dirty black hat. His face was filthy and he stared at Tuff with bloodshot eyes.

"Judge June said the General would have a brigade of soldiers," Tuff said to Sadie. "There are only two armed guards on this wagon train. No soldiers. That cowboy has the eyes of an outlaw."

The door to the wagon swung open. "Meet General Muster," said the Wagon Boss.

With a big grunt, the General bounded out. He was short, with a filthy black beard. He wore a coonskin cap with a dark-brown shirt and britches. Gray snakeskin boots finished off his outfit.

"Howdy," said the General. "Are you Judge June's Deputies? You're too young, only a couple of kids. Judge June said there might be one or two unfriendlies between here and Muleshoe and she sent children. Probably not her best idea. Glad I decided to disguise

myself as a Mountain Man. I've got the US Army brigade coming. They're a little way behind us."

Oh, thought Tuff. *That's why he doesn't have any soldiers. But is he really the General?* Then Tuff noticed the two big silver Colt 45s that gleamed in the General's double holsters. *He's an Army man, for sure,* he thought.

"Are you sure that's General Muster, Tuff?" Sadie whispered.

"I think so." Tuff saw Silver Heels' ears prick up. "Look, Sadie. He senses trouble."

"YEE-HAW!" A gray figure on a dark horse galloped up. "Here you go, General, how about a slap on the back?"

"It's an ambush," called out the Wagon Boss. He snapped his whip at the rider, who reached down, punched the General on the arm then rode off into the scrub trees.

"It was Little Nose George," shouted Tuff. "He must have been the one who circled us at camp last night. He followed us here."

"Oh, no. The General's been hurt," said Sadie.

Tuff and Sadie jumped off their horses and ran over to General Muster.

"I'm OK, its not too serious," the General said as he rolled up his sleeve. "Only a little nick in the arm. I thought you two were supposed to protect me."

"I think we should have a doctor look at the wound," said Sadie. "It might be worse than you think."

"Did you say it was Little Nose George who hit me?" snapped General Muster. "Wait till I get my hands on that bandit."

"Sorry I missed him, General," said the

Wagon Boss. He shouted at the black-hatted cowboy. "Hey numbskull. You're supposed to protect us."

"Oops," the cowboy said with a sneer. "I guess I'm sorry."

"Let's go," said Tuff. "Not only do we have to get the General to a doctor, we only have one day to get through the Sand Hills."

Sadie said, "Relax. Let's follow Judge June's map, stay on the trail and head straight for Muleshoe. With any luck we'll be there by lunchtime tomorrow."

Tuff said, "General, I hope we get you all the way to Muleshoe. Are you comfortable and set to go?"

"We're good to go, as soon as this sling gets into place," answered the General with a frown. The Wagon Boss carefully put a sling around the General's arm.

As they mounted up and started to move, the Wagon Boss said with a worried voice, "I know General Muster well. I think he's hurt bad, but he won't show it. We need a doctor soon."

Oh dear, Tuff thought.

CHAPTER FIVE

A DETOUR TO NO-TREES TOWN

The heat of the summer sun meant they often had to stop so the horses and mules could have a rest. The wagon train rolled along the muddy ruts in the trail up through the Sand Hills. It was so hot the mud sizzled.

Sadie was the first to notice a shimmering light in the distance.

"What's that?" she asked. "It looks like the sun reflected off a piece of metal."

As they got closer, they saw a signpost with a metal sign. It gleamed in the hot midday sun.

On the sign was written:

WELCOME 2 TO NO-TREES TOWN

we don't hav trees but we r home to a SHADY SALOON, lots of wunderful people + a few old SOREHEADS turn off the trail and follow the road ↗ SOWTH!

Soon after the first sign, they saw another:

Sadie said, "Free sarsaparilla would be mighty nice on a hot day like this."

Tuff checked the map. "Judge June's map doesn't show a town named No-Trees. This is strange."

"Well, you know how fast new towns pop up around the Wild West these days," said

Sadie. "A lot of people from the east settled here. Maybe Judge June's map is out of date."

"Judge June's maps are never out of date," said Tuff.

They looked up as the wagon train drew alongside.

"Deputies, it looks like there's a town nearby. The General's arm is worse. Should we see if there's a doctor in the town?" asked the Wagon Boss.

"The town isn't on our map," said Tuff. "I'm not sure who we might find. They do seem friendly from their signs."

"The cowboy says he's heard of the town. He says the people of No-Trees are nice," said the Wagon Boss.

Tuff stared at the cowboy.

"Just a minute," Tuff said, "I'd like to talk this over with Sadie." They trotted Silver Heels and Jenny over to a shady spot under a big live oak tree.

"Sadie, I'm worried. Judge June told us

to stay on the trail. Should we turn off to a town that doesn't even appear on her map? Plus the cowboy was supposed to guard the General, but he let Little Nose George get close enough to club him. I don't trust that cowboy one bit."

"But the General needs a doctor and our job is to get him safely to Muleshoe. No doctor and we might lose him to his wound. I think the cowboy seems harmless enough."

"I think the cowboy's like a dog who doesn't look fierce 'till he bites you," said Tuff.

"I don't think we have a choice. The General might not last until nightfall. We must see if there is a doc in No-Trees," Sadie said.

"Alright then," said Tuff as he relaxed a bit. "Besides I'm also thirsty for an ice-cold sarsaparilla."

Sadie grinned as they rode back to the General's wagon train.

"Let's head into No-Trees," said Tuff. "We hope we find a doc there. If we don't, at least we'll get out of this heat for a while."

"Good idea," said the Wagon Boss.

The cowboy sneered, "Yeah, good idea, Sheriff; it's the right thing to do, ha ha."

"Watch it cowboy," Sadie snapped. "We'll ride behind you and the General into town."

As they turned off the Goodnight-Loving Trail toward No-Trees, Tuff fingered his bullwhip.

"Let's be ready for trouble," Sadie whispered. Her sharp black eyes looked dead ahead.

"We will be."

CHAPTER SIX

MY NAME IS SAM BASS

The wagon train bumped down the road to No-Trees Town.

"We're moving about as fast as a herd of turtles," said Sadie. "We might never get to that sarsaparilla."

Tuff pointed out what seemed like a million black-eared jackrabbits.

"Yuk," said Sadie. "I think jackrabbits are

awful. They're full of ticks and mites. If you get near them they make you sick. You can get Rocky Mountain spotted fever from them."

"I'm not surprised to see all the animals. Look how green it is. There's a lake," Tuff said.

The land around them was full of green trees. A small lake lay ahead.

On the other side of the lake was a group of buildings. Signs hung on them. There was a saloon, a General Store, a hotel and a Telegraph Office. A sign at the town's edge said:

Welcome to No-Trees
Make your way to the saloon
for a cold sarsaparilla

Not a person was in sight. The only sound was the "buzz buzz" of the cicadas.

"It's odd," Tuff said. "Where are the people? There aren't any houses."

The wagon train drove around the lake and stopped in the middle of the little town.

"There's no sign of anybody," Tuff said. "Let's go into the saloon and see if anyone's there."

Tuff and Sadie dismounted from their horses. They grabbed their saddlebags. As they walked up to the saloon the batwing doors flew open and out came a laughing cowboy.

He wore a dirty black hat and had bloodshot eyes.

"Welcome to No-Trees folks, where we like to joke," he cried. "We call our little town No-Trees, but it's full of trees, ha ha."

"What a funny joke," said Sadie, who wasn't laughing. "We have a serious problem. One of us has a bad wound and we need a doctor."

"You're in luck, ponytails," said the cowboy. "There's a doc right inside the saloon. My name is Larry but everybody calls me 'Laughing' Larry 'cause I'm always laughing, ha ha."

Tuff looked over at the cowboy riding with the Wagon Boss. He saw him wink at Laughing Larry.

Tuff, Sadie and the Wagon Boss followed Laughing Larry into the saloon. The saloon

smelled like a slimy pile of dead eels. A cockroach scurried across the floor.

A single person sat at the wooden bar. He wore a dirty black hat. His face was scaly, like a fish. His nasty green bloodshot eyes stared at Tuff and Sadie.

"Hello, Deputy Sadie and Sheriff Tuff," he

said. "My name is Sam Bass. Welcome to my little town. How about a nice cold sarsaparilla? We built No-Trees Town as a trick to get you here. You fell for it."

The batwing doors burst open. In came General Muster, followed by his "guard" the cowboy, who had the General's holsters plus his two big silver Colts.

"Well, look who we have here," said Sam Bass. "If it isn't my old pal General 'Buster' Muster. The Mountain-Man disguise can't fool me."

"Now listen to me, Sam," said the General. "I'm hurt pretty bad. We can talk later. Right now, I need a doctor."

The two cowboys joined Sam Bass at the bar.

"Hand over that bullwhip of yours, Sheriff Brunson," said Sam Bass as the rest of his gang crowded into the saloon. "You too, Deputy Marcus."

Tuff and Sadie handed their bullwhips to Sam Bass and the cowboy who rode with the General's wagon train took the Wagon Boss' whip. "I knew you were up to no good," Tuff said to the cowboy. "You worked for Sam Bass all along."

"Oh, don't be a crybaby, Tuff," sneered Laughing Larry. "My brother here, he wants to have a bit of fun, ha ha."

"Keep quiet," growled Sam at the two laughing cowboys. "I do all the talking in this gang."

"What do you want from us, Sam?" asked Sadie.

"From you?" answered Sam. "I don't want

nothing. From your boss, Judge June, I'd like a lot."

"She won't give you a thing, Sam Bass. She doesn't care a hoot about outlaws."

"I bet she cares when I tell her I have her sheriff, his deputy and General Muster of the United States Army as my prisoners," said Sam. "If she wants you back alive, my guess is she'll give me the whole town of Muleshoe. I'll turn all the hideout kids into outlaws. The outlaw army will take over."

"You'll never take over Muleshoe," Tuff said. "We won't let you."

"You and your deputy have got no bullwhips, Tuff. You can't stop anybody," laughed Sam Bass, as the two cowboy brothers grinned along with him. "Throw these prisoners into the dungeon."

CHAPTER SEVEN

SAWBONES TURNS TAIL

Tuff, Sadie, General Muster and the Wagon Boss were put in the dungeon behind the saloon, a filthy room with no windows.

Tuff had never felt so hopeless. He looked through a crack in the wall at the rest of Sam Bass's gang. There were at least twenty more outlaws.

I feel dumb to have fallen for Sam Bass's trick, he said to himself.

"Doctor," moaned
the General. "Somebody
get me a doctor."

Sadie knelt down next to the General and called out to Sam Bass, who stood outside the dungeon door.

"Please get us a doctor. The General might not make it through the night."

"OK, don't complain, ponytails," Sam said. He grabbed one of his henchmen. "Go fetch Sawbones. The General is worth more to us alive."

A short time later, Dr. Joe "Sawbones" Newton arrived. He examined General Muster then said, "I'm glad I got here in time. He'll be fine. Hand me my saddlebags. It's where I keep all my medicines and tools."

Sawbones wore an eye patch. "What happened to your right eye?" Sadie asked.

"Lost it last week," Sawbones said. "But I'll find it again soon. Might have rolled under my bed."

"Eww," Sadie said.

Sawbones got out one of his surgical instruments. "How long have you been a doctor?" the General asked. "You're a kid, like Tuff and Sadie. Will this hurt?"

"Maybe, if I slip a bit while you're gabbing.

Please keep quiet," Sawbones said. "You only ask 'cause you never saw a black doctor before, did you?"

Tuff decided he liked Sawbones. "Can I ask a question? Do you really saw people's bones?" Tuff said.

"Only if their name is Sam Bass," the doctor said.

"What? Aren't you part of Sam Bass's gang?" Sadie asked.

"I was," Sawbones said. "Sam still thinks I am." He lowered his voice as he said, "I'm about to turn tail on him."

"Why?" asked Sadie. "Don't you make lots of money in Sam Bass's gang?"

"Sam Bass is nothing but a bully," said Sawbones as he worked on the General's wound. "He only picks fights with people who can't defend themselves, like the wounded General. My family were slaves back in Alabama. I know all about bullies. It's why I left home for the Wild West."

"Why did you join the outlaw gang?" Tuff asked.

"Because the only people who would let a black doctor work on them were the outlaws," Sawbones replied. "I'm tired of them though. I don't like bullies. I'm on your side now."

"You can work on me anytime, Sawbones. I feel better already," said the General as he sat up. "How will we get out of this dungeon?"

Tuff said, "I've thought about it. It's getting dark outside, almost sundown. Maybe we can trick Sam Bass and his gang."

"Trick Sam Bass? He's one of the cleverest outlaws in the whole Wild West," said General Muster.

"Maybe he's not as clever as he thinks he is," said Tuff. "Remember, all these teenage outlaws brag that they're a genius. Sawbones, let me ask you something in secret."

Tuff leaned over and whispered a question to Sawbones.

Sawbones grinned and nodded.

"I have one other question," said Tuff. "Can we borrow scissors, a needle and thread from you?"

"Of course," said Sawbones. "I always carry extra in case any of my patients talk too much. If they do I sew their mouth shut."

"Sadie, can you please give your saddlebags to Sawbones?" Tuff said.

"Sure," Sadie replied and handed them over.

"Gather around, everybody," Tuff said. He lowered his voice as he whispered his plan.

"Good plan, Tuff," said the General. "How do we know Sam Bass will fall for it?"

"Because he trusts Sawbones and believes anything he says," said Tuff. "When we put the plan into action, he'll be like cotton candy in our hands. Don't forget it's about to be pitch black outside. The dark night will work in our favor."

"For this plan to work, one of us must escape from the dungeon before the others," said the General. "Who can escape first?"

Sadie smiled and winked.

"Leave that part to me," she said.

CHAPTER EIGHT

ESCAPE FROM THE DUNGEON

Sam Bass and his gang laughed around the campfire after their supper of wild hogs and fried prickly pear cactus.

Sam called out, "Hey Sawbones, did you fix the poor little General yet?"

"Yeah, Sawbones," said Laughing Larry. "Maybe you can sew a new face on him. The one he's got sure is ugly."

"Those prisoners are toast," shouted Sam as his gang roared with laughter. "After Judge June gives us everything we want, we'll throw them off Buffalo Cliff."

Buffalo Cliff, thought Tuff. *Oh no.*

Inside the dungeon, Sawbones picked through Sadie's saddlebags and found the white bed-sheets. He picked up the scissors, threaded his needle and went to work.

"There you go, Tuff," he said when he finished. "Hope these do the trick."

"Thanks, Sawbones. Once the fire dies out the gang will be fast asleep," whispered Tuff. "Just before dawn it'll be time to make our move."

"OK," said Sawbones. "I'll go out now to talk with Sam Bass. Hope this works."

Tuff looked through the crack in the wall. He watched as Sawbones opened the dungeon door and walked over to the campfire.

"Hey, Sam," said Sawbones. "It doesn't look good for the General. He's hurt real bad."

"Poor dear," said Sam as the gang all smiled.

"Also, Tuff, Sadie and the Wagon Boss look real sick. I think they got the Rocky Mountain spotted fever from those jackrabbits," said Sawbones.

"Poor dears," laughed Sam Bass as the gang all whooped and hollered.

"It could be none of them stays alive till morning," said Sawbones.

"Poor little dears," yelled Sam Bass as the gang laughed so hard they had tears in their eyes.

"Let's get some shut-eye," Sam said. "We've got a real fun day ahead of us tomorrow."

Sam told Laughing Larry to guard the door of the dungeon.

While Larry stood guard, the Deputies watched through the crack in the dungeon wall until the fire died out. The gang finally went to sleep.

Tuff and Sadie lay down on the dusty

dungeon floor. The General and the Wagon Boss were already asleep.

It was almost morning, still pitch black outside, when Tuff whispered, "It's time."

"Wish me luck," Sadie said. "I'm going out the door." She stood up.

"Sadie?" said Tuff through the crack in the wall. "Where did you go?"

"I'm here," whispered Sadie from outside the crack. "Pretty fast aren't I?"

"Wow," said Tuff. "You went right through the door. Judge June's magic worked."

"That was amazing. I never walked right through a door before," Sadie said.

"OK," Tuff said. "Whisper to me when you get into your costume. I'll wake the General and the Wagon Boss then give the signal."

He woke the General and the Wagon Boss and whispered, "Sadie's out. Let's get into our costumes, quick." They put on their costumes.

Tuff heard Sadie whisper, "I'm ready."

"Are you ready too?" Tuff asked General Muster and the Wagon Boss.

"We are," said General Muster.

"WOOOOOOOO!" hollered Tuff, as loud as he could.

"YEEEEOOOOWWWWW!" shouted the General and the Wagon Boss.

The dungeon door flew open. Laughing Larry's jaw dropped when he saw the three ghosts.

"Boss," he yelled to Sam Bass. "Wake up. The prisoners are gone. Only ghosts are in the dungeon. Oh, no, look, one of them is floating right above the campfire."

Sadie floated in her white ghost bed-sheet costume in the center of the camp, where the campfire had been. Above her, Judge June's familiar, a gray owl, batted his wings and hooted loudly.

"BOOOOOOOOO!" Sadie yelled.

"Those ghosts are real," yelled Sawbones.

"Run for it, Sam."

"Run for your life," shouted Sam Bass. "The prisoners turned into ghosts. One of 'em even turned into an owl."

Sam Bass and his gang sprinted for their horses and sped away into the desert as Sadie, Tuff, the General and the Wagon Boss hollered lots of "BOO"s and "WOO"s.

The sun rose over the lake as Tuff grabbed his and Sadie's bullwhips. The General smiled as he holstered his big Colts and handed the Wagon Boss his whip.

"What a great plan, Tuff," said Sawbones. "I told you Sam Bass was terrified of ghosts."

"Glad you had those sheets, Sadie," Tuff said as she joined them on the ground. "Let's get out of this ruckus and head home to Muleshoe."

They ran to the wagon train.

"Deputies, ride inside the wagon with me. The Wagon Boss will tie Silver Heels and Jenny to the back," General Muster said. "Sawbones, why don't you ride up top so you can keep the Wagon Boss company?"

Sawbones nodded and climbed on the wagon roof. Tuff, Sadie and the General smiled as they jumped up inside the wagon.

They soon quit smiling as they stared down the blue-steel barrels of an ultra delux, super spray, mega soaker water gun.

"Good mornin'," said Big Nose George Parrot, as he cocked the gun. "Ready to go swimmin'?"

CHAPTER NINE

PARROT WINGS ARE CLIPPED

"Nice to meet you, General," said Big Nose George, "even though we won't know each other long, seein' as how this might be the wettest day of your life. That Mountain Man disguise is dumb. I might mistake you for a big ole bear and soak you. Now hand over those silver Colts, nice and slow."

"I'm not afraid of you, Parrot," said the

General as he took out his pistols. "All I have
to do is give a whistle and my Wagon Boss
will jump down on you like an anteater on
an ant."

"How's he gonna jump down on me?" Big Nose George laughed. "Hey George."

Little Nose George appeared at the window.

"Got those two ragamuffins tied up yet?" said Big Nose George.

"Yup," said Little Nose George. "I've got little sis guardin' 'em."

Oh dear, thought Tuff, *they've got the whole outlaw family here, even Tiny Nose Peggy.*

"Start up the wagon, Tiny Nose Peggy," yelled Big Nose George. "Head for Buffalo Cliff. I wanna see if these Dep-u-ties can fly like us Parrots. Ha ha ha. Now gimme yore bullwhip, sheriff."

"Parrots always have their wings clipped," said Tuff as he handed over his whip. "You'll never get us over Buffalo Cliff."

Big Nose George raised the water rifle and pointed it at Sheriff Tuff.

"You know what," he snarled. "I'm tired enough of this smarty pants sheriff. I'm gonna serve him his water fountain right now."

Tuff glanced at Sadie. *Big Nose George forgot she had a bullwhip too.*

As Tuff hoped, she lifted her jacket slightly.

Tuff's hand was inches from her whip.

If she could distract Big Nose George, Tuff thought.

"Hey, look out there," Sadie shouted. "Jackrabbits."

Big Nose George turned to look out the window. "So what? Are you hungry? Ha ha."

"Hey," he shouted when he turned back. "What the –?"

"Look out you dirty outlaw, here comes Sheriff Tuff Brunson!" Tuff grabbed Sadie's bullwhip.

"CRACK!"

He snapped it quickly around Big Nose George's wrists.

"I'll take that mega soaker," Tuff said as he stuffed a red bandana into Big Nose George's mouth. "Guess you'll have to stop your chirping now, Parrot."

Tuff handed the General his silver Colts and he and Sadie hopped up out the window as the wagon sped up.

They surprised Little Nose George and Tiny Nose Peggy, handcuffed their wrists and untied the Wagon Boss and Sawbones who then tucked the outlaws in the luggage bin of the wagon.

"Nice work, Tuff," said General Muster. "One of these days you'll have to tell me how you do it."

"Do what?" said Tuff.

"Make yourself invisible."

"Oh, I don't make myself invisible. I'm fast, so fast you can't see me," Tuff said as he winked at Sadie.

"Speaking of fast, we'll be home by lunchtime," Tuff said as he looked out the window. He was happy to see the sign:

Surely a half-mile is too short for any more trouble? he wondered.

THE BIG SPRING
a HARF-MILE aheyd

DANGEя!

GIANT POYSONOUS
PRICKLY PEAЯ CACTI
KEEP OWT!

CHAPTER TEN

WELCOME TO MULESHOE, GENERAL MUSTER

"Hey, what's this?" General Muster said as they neared the oasis called The Big Spring. "There isn't a town here. It's a giant prickly pear cactus forest."

"Don't worry," Tuff said. "I'll hop on Silver Heels. Follow me."

Tuff mounted up on Silver Heels and

led the way. He watched General Muster and the Wagon Boss blink as the cacti turned to beautiful green trees with bright yellow flowers.

Sawbones whispered to Sadie, "Cactus? What was the General talking about? I only saw the green trees, a blue lake and now here's the town."

Sadie smiled at Sawbones. "Only children can find Muleshoe. That's why you could see it and the General couldn't. It's a hideout for kids."

Judge June was waiting for them in the main street.

"Welcome to Muleshoe, General Muster," she said.

"I'm mighty glad to be here," said the General. "Without your sheriff and his deputy, we wouldn't

have made it safely. The United States Army will be at The Big Spring in a couple of hours. The new US Army Camp will be called Camp Beak."

"I'm so happy to see you guys," said Judge June to Tuff and Sadie as she and Sawbones jumped down off the General's wagon train. "I hope you didn't have any trouble. Who's your new friend?"

"Not much," Tuff said. "Only one or two little scrapes. Our new friend's name is Joe Newton. He's a doctor. His nickname is Sawbones."

"Hello, Sawbones, nice to meet you," Judge June said with a smile. "The hideout kids need a doctor in Muleshoe. Would you like the job?"

"Yes. I'd love the job," Sawbones replied. "Thanks Judge June."

"Good. I'll make you a deputy as well," said Judge June. "Congratulations Tuff and Sadie. I have a bit of bad news, I'm afraid," she continued, as she turned toward Tuff.

"What is it?" asked Tuff.

"While you were away, Big Nose George escaped from jail," said Judge June.

"Oh dear," said Tuff, as he grinned at Sadie. "How did he get out?"

"Well, as you know, when you're away, I have Deputy Dan guard the jailhouse," said Judge June. "Yesterday Deputy Dan had four plates of burritos and tacos for lunch. After lunch he sat down a the rocking chair next to a jail cell then fell fast asleep."

"Nothing wrong with the story so far," said Tuff. "I often have a nap in my chair after a big lunch of burritos and tacos."

"Yes, Tuff, but *you* don't fall asleep with the keys to the jail hanging out of your pocket."

"Oh," said Tuff. "So I guess Big Nose George reached through the bars, grabbed the keys, then lickety-split, off he went."

"Exactly," said Judge June. "I also have good news though. We captured Little Nose

George and Tiny Nose Peggy. They're locked up in jail."

"Oh, is that so?" said Sadie with a giggle.

"I've got Jelly Roll Jim and a posse on a search for Big Nose George right now," Judge June added. "I'm sure they'll bring him in soon."

Deputy Dan walked up. He looked sheepish.

"Judge June," he said. "I have a bit more bad news."

"What is it?" said Judge June.

"I checked the jail. Little Nose George and Tiny Nose Peggy are not in their cells. They've flown the coop," said Deputy Dan.

"No," said Judge June, glaring at Deputy Dan. "I ought to -"

Tuff and Sadie grinned at each other.

"Judge June, can you please come over to the wagon train?" said Sadie.

"Sure," said Judge June as she walked over. "Why?"

Judge June looked in the wagon and saw the faces of Big Nose George, Little Nose George and Tiny Nose Peggy. Their hands were in handcuffs. They whimpered and cried like teeny babies with tummy aches.

"Well, well," Judge June exclaimed. "Nice work. Let's go get a sarsaparilla."

THE END

Author's Note

The Hideout Kids series of books features several of the same characters, animals, places and things. Here are some brief descriptions:

Charlie "Sir" Ringo: A cowboy detective.

Deputy Joe "Sawbones" Newton: Muleshoe's doctor, a deputy to Sheriff Tuff Brunson.

Deputy Sadie Marcus: Ten-year-old deputy of Muleshoe and Tuff's best friend.

Hooter: Judge June's familiar. An owl-shaped spirit who helps Judge June practice her magic.

Jelly Roll Jim, Toothless Tom, Deputy Dan Pigeon: Teenagers who grew up in Muleshoe and stayed on to help Judge June and the Hideout Kids.

Jenny: Sadie's Horse. A gift from Chief Ten Bears of the Comanche Tribe Indians.

Judge Junia "June" Beak: United States District Judge of the West. She is also a good and powerful witch.

Miss Hannah Humblebee: A Hopi Tribe Indian girl detective.

Mr. Zip: Tuff's pet. A beaver.

Muleshoe, Texas: Home of the Hideout Kids. Only children can find it and live there.

S'mores: Chocolate-covered marshmallows, served on sugar crackers. Dee-lish.

Sarsaparilla: The most popular soft drink of the Wild West. It's thought to have healing powers and is made from the root of the sarsaparilla vine. Yummy.

Sheriff Tuff Brunson: Ten-year-old sheriff of Muleshoe.

Silver Heels: Tuff's horse. Also a gift from Chief Ten Bears.

Spiky: A giant saguaro cactus that guards The Cave.

The Cave: A magical place where the kids can travel through time.

The Singing Cowboy Poet: A magical elf.

Wild Thing: Judge June's pet. A pink fairy armadillo.

Here are descriptions of a few animals and plants which you might not have seen before, and which appear in this book:

Cabrito: Barbequed goat.

Coyote: A prairie wolf.

Jackrabbits: Wild desert hares.

Mesquite trees: Typical tree of the Texas desert.

GRIZZLY BEARS & BEAVER PELTS

Chapter One

APRIL FOOLS

It was a warm spring afternoon in the Wild West Texas town of Muleshoe.

Sheriff Tuff Brunson nodded off in his rocking chair. He had just finished a delicious lunch of tacos and burritos.

As Tuff fell asleep, he heard the tiny cowboy poet singing. The song drifted in through the jailhouse window:

Chief Black Bear's gang
Trapped a Mountain Man
Though the gang was small
They had a great plan

'Cause the giant Mountain Men
Have just one scare
They fear nothing in the world
'Cept a giant grizzly bear

Just behind Tuff, locked inside a cell, was the meanest outlaw in the Wild West, "Big Nose" George Parrot. Big Nose George was sound asleep too.

"BAM!" "SLAM!" "KERPOW!" came a pounding on the door to the jailhouse.

"What the –?" Tuff said as his eyes struggled open.

"What made that noise?" he said to Deputy Dan, his assistant jailer. "Open the door and let's have a look."

Deputy Dan let out a loud "SNORE!" and

stayed fast asleep in his own rocking chair. Deputy Dan always ate twice as many tacos and burritos as Tuff. His snore was soon followed by a loud "BURP!"

Amazing. He even burps in his sleep, thought Tuff.

"You're impossible to wake up," Tuff said to Deputy Dan. "Sadie," he yelled.

Deputy Sadie Marcus ran into the room from her jailhouse office.

"Did you hear that noise?" Tuff asked her.

"Of course I did," said Sadie. "Someone, or something, was pounding on the door. Let's have a look outside and see what's going on."

"Is your bullwhip ready?" Tuff asked.

"Yep," Sadie said as her fingers curled around the handle of her whip.

Tuff checked the leather bullwhip hanging from his belt before he carefully cracked the door open. He and Sadie peeped outside.

"Good afternoon," said a voice from

somewhere near the door. "Would you like to buy some cakes today?"

"No, we don't want any cakes," Tuff said, looking around.

"Then how about some candies?" said the voice.

"No candies either," said Tuff, still trying to see who was talking.

"Ice cream?" said the voice.

"No," said Tuff.

"Would you like to see who this is?" said the voice. "Step outside; it's a surprise."

Tuff whispered to Sadie, "Hey, today is the first of April. I think it's Jelly Roll Jim. He's playing an April Fools' joke on us. Let's play along and go out."

The two law officers stepped outside the door.

"Ha ha, you're trapped," said the voice as a rope net came down on them from above. They struggled to break free but they couldn't move.

"You thought this was April Fools but the joke's on you," shouted "Little Nose" George Parrot, Big Nose George's younger brother.

"Yeah Sheriff," squeaked "Tiny Nose" Peggy Parrot, the youngest member of the outlaw Parrot Gang. "Nah, nah, ha, ha. Happy April Fools' Day, 'cept we're not your friends and we don't care if you're happy."

"Listen, you pretty Parrots," said Tuff. "Get this net off us right now or you'll spend the rest of your lives eating bird food, locked up inside the jail with your smelly brother."

"We'll see who's gonna be locked up, Sheriff," said Little Nose George. "Peggy, grab the keys off Deputy Dan and let's do a jail cell switcheroo. Big Nose George out, the two Dep-u-ties in."

"Wake up, Deputy Dan," Tuff yelled. "We need your help."

"SNORE!" came the sound from Deputy Dan's rocking chair. "BURP!"

Peggy and Little Nose George headed into the jailhouse.

"I don't know, Sadie," Tuff said. "Even an explosion couldn't wake up Deputy Dan!"

Wait. Explosion. Tuff remembered some thing very important. He smiled to himself.

"Hang on, Little Nose Peggy-Bird brain," Tuff said. "Deputy Dan doesn't have the keys. They're in my desk drawer."

Tuff grinned as Tiny Nose Peggy and Little Nose George jumped over to the desk and yanked the drawer open.

"POP!" A booby trap exploded, spraying sleeping gas in the two outlaws' faces. They quickly fell to the ground, fast asleep from the gas.

"What the –?" said Deputy Dan as he leapt out of his chair. "Tuff, why are you and Sadie wrapped up in a net?" he asked, rubbing his eyes.

"You were wrong, Tuff." Sadie smiled. "An explosion *did* wake up Deputy Dan."

"Get this net off us, Deputy Dan," Tuff said. "Let's tie up those two clipped Parrots before they fly around causing more of a ruckus."

MIKE GLEASON

HIDEOUT KIDS

TUFF, SADIE &
THE WILD WEST

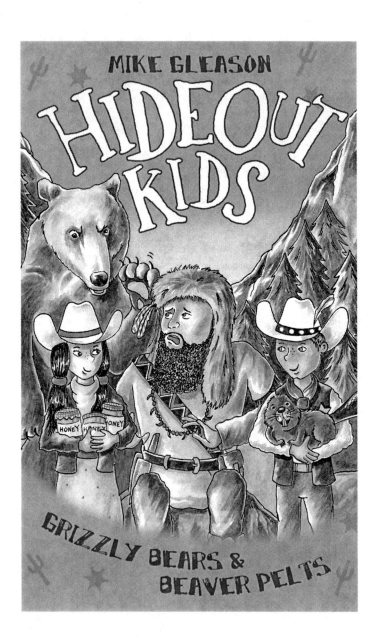

ABOUT THE AUTHOR

Hideout Kids author Mike Gleason comes from a small town in Texas. He grew up with cowboys, cowgirls and exciting stories of Wild West adventures. He was a wildcatter in the Texas oil fields and a board director at MGM in Hollywood. He created and produced an award-winning music television series at Abbey Road Studios. He lives and writes in London.

ABOUT THE ILLUSTRATOR

Hideout Kids illustrator Victoria Taylor comes from Cheltenham, England, and her love of art was inspired by her maternal grandmother. She trained at Plymouth University and worked for many years as a graphic designer. Having returned to her first love of painting and drawing, Victoria is now a freelance book illustrator. She lives in Gloucestershire with her husband and two children.